of co-ordination
is both valuable and
important to a child's later
development, and this is found,
for instance, in *Finger Rhymes*,
the first book of the six book series.

This series provides an enjoyable intro-
duction to poetry, music and dance for
every young child. Most books of this
type have only a few rhymes for each
age group, whereas each book of this
series is intended for a particular age
group. There is a strong teaching sequence
in the selection of rhymes, from the
first simple ways of winning the child's
interest by toe tapping and palm
tickling jingles, through practice in
numbers, memory and pronunciation,
to combining sound, action and
words. For the first time young
children can learn rhymes
in a sequence that is
related

Contents

LEARNING WITH TRADITIONAL RHYMES

Number Rhymes

by DOROTHY and JOHN TAYLOR
with illustrations by BRIAN PRICE THOMAS
and photographs by JOHN MOYES

Ladybird Books Ltd Loughborough 1976

One, two, three, four

One, two, three, four,
Mary at the cottage door,
Five, six, seven, eight,
Eating cherries off a plate.

One, two, kittens that mew

One, two, kittens that mew,
Two, three, birds on a tree,
Three, four, shells on the shore,
Four, five, bees from the hive,
Five, six, the cow that licks,
Six, seven, rooks in the heaven
Seven, eight, sheep at the gate,
Eight, nine, clothes on a line,
Nine, ten, the little black hen.

John Brown had a little soldier

John Brown had a little soldier,
John Brown had a little soldier,
John Brown had a little soldier,
One little soldier boy.
He had one little, two little, three little soldiers,
Four little, five little, six little soldiers,
Seven little, eight little, nine little soldiers,
Ten little soldier boys.

John Brown had ten little soldiers,
John Brown had ten little soldiers,
John Brown had ten little soldiers,
Ten little soldier boys.
He had ten little, nine little, eight little soldiers,
Seven little, six little, five little soldiers,
Four little, three little, two little soldiers,
One little soldier boy.

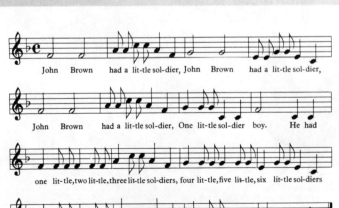

John Brown had a lit-tle sol-dier, John Brown had a lit-tle sol-dier,

John Brown had a lit-tle sol-dier, One lit-tle sol-dier boy. He had

one lit-tle, two lit-tle, three lit-tle sol-diers, four lit-tle, five lit-tle, six lit-tle sol-diers

sev'n lit-tle, eight lit-tle, nine lit-tle sol-diers, ten lit-tle sol-dier boys.

1, 2,
Buckle my shoe;

3, 4,
Knock at the door;

5, 6,
Pick up sticks;

7, 8,
Lay them straight;

9, 10,
A big fat hen;

11, 12,
Dig and delve;

10

13, 14,
Maids a-courting;

15, 16,
Maids in the kitchen;

17, 18,
Maids in waiting;

19, 20,
My plate's empty.

This old man, he played one

This old man, he played one,
He played nick-nack on my drum.

Nick-nack paddy whack,
Give a dog a bone,
This old man came rolling home.

This old man, he played two,
He played nick-nack on my shoe.

Nick-nack paddy whack, etc.

This old man, he played three,
He played nick-nack on my knee.

This old man, he played four,
He played nick-nack on my door.

This old man, he played five,
He played nick-nack on my hive.

This old man, he played six,
He played nick-nack on my sticks.

Nick-nack paddy whack, etc.

This old man, he played seven,
He played nick-nack on my Devon.

This old man, he played eight,
He played nick-nack on my plate.

This old man, he played nine,
He played nick-nack on my line.

This old man, he played ten,
He played nick-nack on my hen.

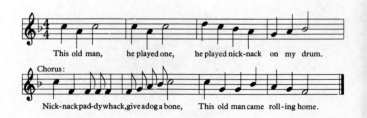

This old man, he played one, he played nick-nack on my drum.

Chorus:

Nick-nack pad-dy whack, give a dog a bone, This old man came roll-ing home.

Music and words reprinted by permission of Faber Music Ltd. (for J. Curwen & Sons Ltd.)

One I love, two I love

One I love, two I love,
Three I love, I say;
Four I love with all my heart,
Five I cast away.
Six he loves, seven she loves,
Eight they love together;
Nine he comes, ten he tarries,
Eleven he woos, and twelve he marries.

I love sixpence, jolly little sixpence

I love sixpence, jolly little sixpence,
I love sixpence better than my life;
I spent a penny of it, I lent a penny of it,
And I took fourpence home to my wife.

Oh, my little fourpence, jolly little fourpence,
I love fourpence better than my life;
I spent a penny of it, I lent a penny of it,
And I took twopence home to my wife.

Oh, my little twopence, jolly little twopence,
I love twopence better than my life;
I spent a penny of it, I lent a penny of it,
And I took nothing home to my wife.

Oh, my little nothing, jolly little nothing,
What will nothing buy for my wife?
I have nothing, I spend nothing,
I love nothing better than my wife.

I love six - pence, jol - ly lit - tle six - pence,

I love six - pence bet - ter than my life;

I spent a pen - ny of it, I lent a pen - ny of it,

And I took four - pence home to my wife.

19

Seven black friars,
sitting back to back

Seven black friars, sitting back to back,
Fished from the bridge for a pike or a jack.
The first caught a tiddler,
The second caught a crab,
The third caught a winkle,
The fourth caught a dab,
The fifth caught a tadpole,
The sixth caught an eel,
The seventh one caught an old cart-wheel.

Chook, chook, chook, chook, chook

Chook, chook, chook, chook, chook,
Good morning, Mrs Hen,
How many chickens have you got?
Madam, I've got ten.
Four of them are yellow,
And four of them are brown.
And two of them are speckled red,
The nicest in the town.

There were two wrens upon a tree

There were two wrens upon a tree,
Whistle and I'll come to thee;
Another came, and there were three,
Whistle and I'll come to thee;
Another came and there were four,
You needn't whistle any more,
For being frightened, off they flew,
And there are none to show to you.

Ten in the bed

There were ten in the bed,
And the little one said:
"Roll over! Roll over!"
So they all rolled over,
And one fell out.

There were *nine* in the bed
There were *eight* in the bed, etc.

There was one in the bed,
And the little one said:
"Roll over, roll over!"
So he rolled right over and fell right out.

There were none in the bed, so no one said:
"Roll over! Roll over!"

There were ten in the bed, And the lit - tle one said: "Roll
o - ver! Roll o - ver!" So they all rolled o-ver, and one fell out.

Knock, knock, knock, knock

Knock, knock, knock, knock –
Hear the knockings four!
Each a knock for someone standing
At our kitchen door.

The first is a beggar man,
The second is a thief,
The third is a pirate,
And the fourth a robber chief.

Close all the windows,
Lock the door, and then
Call for the policeman quick
To catch those four bad men!

A dozen is twelve

A dozen is twelve,
Or four times three.
Half a dozen is six,
As plain as can be.

Bell horses, bell horses

Bell horses, bell horses,
What time of day?
One o'clock, two o'clock,
Three and away.

Bell horses, bell horses,
What time of day?
Two o'clock, three o'clock,
Four and away.

Bell horses, bell horses,
What time of day?
Five o'clock, six o'clock,
Now time to stay.

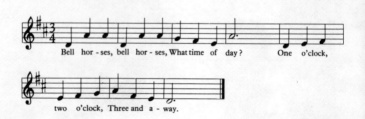

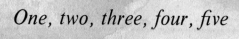

One, two, three, four, five

One, two, three, four, five,
Once I caught a fish alive.
Six, seven, eight, nine, ten,
Then I let it go again.

Why did you let it go?
Because it bit my finger so.
Which finger did it bite?
This little finger on the right.

One for sorrow

One for sorrow,
Two for joy,
Three for a girl,
Four for a boy,
Five for silver,
Six for gold,
Seven for a secret
That is never to be told.

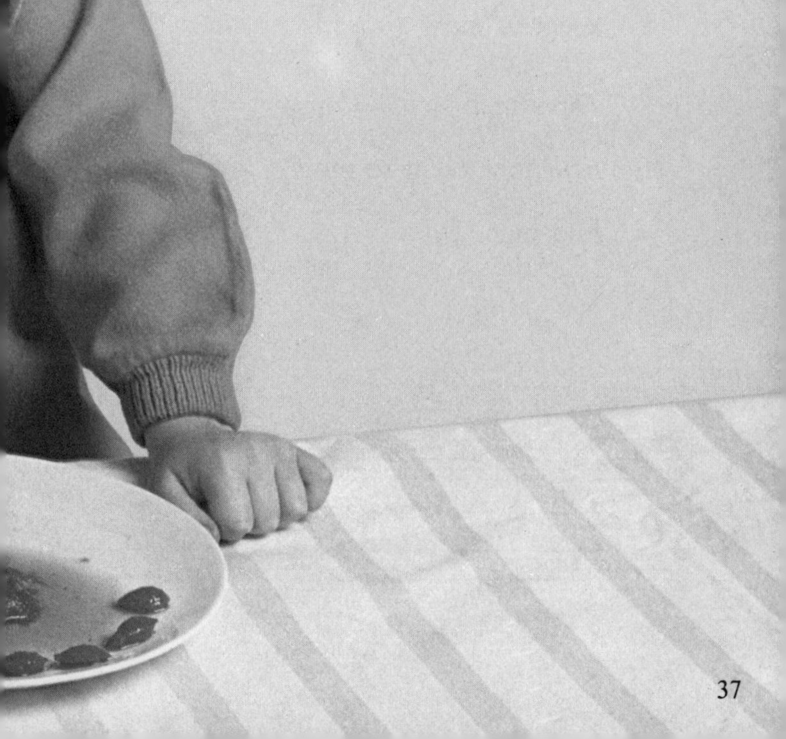

One man went to mow

One man went to mow,
Went to mow a meadow,
One man and his dog,
Went to mow a meadow.

Two men went to mow,
Went to mow a meadow,
Two men, one man and his dog,
Went to mow a meadow.

Three men went to mow,

Four men went to mow,

Five men, *etc.*

One man went to mow, Went to mow a mea-dow,
One man and his dog, Went to mow a mea-dow.

Ten green bottles
hanging on the wall

Ten green bottles hanging on the wall,
Ten green bottles hanging on the wall,
And if one green bottle should accidentally fall
There'd be nine green bottles hanging on the wall.

Nine green bottles hanging on the wall,
Nine green bottles hanging on the wall,
And if one green bottle should accidentally fall
There'd be eight green bottles hanging on the wall.

Eight green bottles, etc., down to

One green bottle hanging on the wall,
One green bottle hanging on the wall,
And if that green bottle should accidentally fall
There'd be no green bottles hanging there at all.

Ten green bot-tles— hang - ing on the wall, Ten green bot-tles— hang-ing on the wall, And if one green bot-tle should ac - ci-dent'lly fall There'd be nine green bot-tles— hang - ing on the wall.

41

The animals came in two by two

The animals came in two by two,
Vive la compagnie.
The centipede with the kangaroo,
Vive la compagnie.

One more river, and that's the river of Jordan,
One more river, there's one more river to cross.

The animals came in three by three,
Vive la compagnie.
The elephant on the back of the flea,
Vive la compagnie.

One more river, etc.

The animals came in four by four,
Vive la compagnie.
The camel he got stuck in the door,
Vive la compagnie.

One more river, etc.

The animals came in five by five,
Some were dead, and some were alive.

The animals came in six by six,
The monkey he was up to his tricks.

The animals came in seven by seven,
Some went to Hell, and some went to Heaven.

The animals came in eight by eight
The worm was early, the bird was late.

The animals came in nine by nine,
Some had water and some had wine.

The animals came in ten by ten,
   Vive la compagnie.
If you want any more you must sing it again,
   Vive la compagnie.

One more river, and that's the river of Jordan,
One more river, there's one more river to cross.

The an-i-mals came in two by two, Vi-ve la com-pag-nie— The
cen-ti-pede with the kan-ga-roo, Vi-ve la com-pag-nie — One more
ri-ver— and that's the ri-ver of Jor-dan—, One more ri-ver— there's
one more ri-ver to cross—.

Chorus

The first day of Christmas

The first day of Christmas,
My true love sent to me:
A partridge in a pear tree.

The second day of Christmas,
My true love sent to me:
Two turtle doves and
A partridge in a pear tree.

The third day of Christmas,
My true love sent to me:
Three French hens, two turtle doves and
A partridge in a pear tree.

The fourth day of Christmas,
My true love sent to me:
Four colly birds, three French hens,
Two turtle doves and
A partridge in a pear tree.

The fifth day of Christmas,
My true love sent to me:
Five gold rings, four colly birds,
Three French hens, two turtle doves and
A partridge in a pear tree.

The sixth day of Christmas . . .
Six geese a-laying, *five gold rings, etc.*

The seventh day of Christmas . . .
Seven swans a-swimming, *six geese a-laying, etc.*

The eighth day of Christmas . . .
Eight maids a-milking, *seven swans a-swimming, etc.*

The ninth day of Christmas . . .
Nine drummers drumming, *eight maids a-milking, etc.*

The tenth day of Christmas . . .
Ten pipers piping, *nine drummers drumming, etc.*

The eleventh day of Christmas . . .
Eleven ladies dancing, *ten pipers piping, etc.*

The twelfth day of Christmas . . .
Twelve lords a-leaping, *eleven ladies dancing, etc.*

50

·❧O❧·

BOOK ONE
Finger Rhymes

A selection of finger counting, face patting, palm tickling and toe tapping rhymes to delight the young child and at the same time exercise his mind and body.

BOOK TWO
Number Rhymes

This book brings together many familiar and some less well known rhymes which help with the first steps of arithmetic: adding, subtracting, multiplying and dividing in their simplest forms.

BOOK THREE
Memory Rhymes

A diverse collection of rhymes mainly concerned with days of the week, months of the year, points of the compass and letters of the alphabet. With these a child learns simple progressions in an amusing and absorbing manner.